Green Bean Books

First published in the UK in 2025 by Green Bean Books

c/o Pen & Sword Books Ltd
George House, Unit 12 & 13, Beevor Street, Off Pontefract Road, Barnsley,
South Yorkshire S71 1HN
www.greenbeanbooks.com

Green Bean edition: 978-1-78438-916-1
Harold Grinspoon Foundation: 978-1-78438-920-8

Designed by Gilad Vitosky
Illustration editor Michal Magen
Edited by Kate Baker, Julie Carpenter and Michael Leventhal
Production by Hugh Allan
Printed in China by Printworks Global Ltd, London and Hong Kong

0325/B2916/A7

FSC
www.fsc.org
FSC® C 007031

# The Curious Case of the Pot Roast

## A Passover Mystery

Written by Jamie Kiffel-Alcheh

Illustrated by Menahem Halberstadt

I zoom down our hallway
to the kitchen, where Mom
is cooking dinner.

"Who invented spoons?" I ask.

"What kind of meal is a matzoh meal?

Can spicy stuff make you breathe fire?"

"What do you want to know *right now*?"
Mom says with a laugh.

"What are you making?" I ask.

"I'm making pot roast for our seder tonight,"
Mom says.

"So she could throw it like a football —
straight into the oven!" calls my uncle from the den.

"No!" says Mom.
"The truth is, I never asked.
But maybe you could!"

I take off
for the stairwell
and hear Mom call out:

"Ancient Egyptians
invented spoons!"
"Thanks!" I call back and
race up one flight of stairs.
I knock on Grandma Shirley's door.

"Got a question?" asks Grandma Shirley.
"Do blueprints come in other colors?" I ask.
"Does anyone live at the top of the Eiffel Tower?
Is that matzoh kugel?"

"What do you want to know *right now?*"
Grandma Shirley says, and laughs.
"Oh yes! Why do you cut off both
ends of a roast?" I ask.

"Because that's how my mother always did it," says Grandma Shirley. "But why did *she* do it?" I ask.

"So she could stick it in her belly button!" calls my grandpa from the living room.

"No!" says Grandma Shirley. "The truth is,
I never asked. But maybe you..."
"I'm on it!" I say, and race toward the stairwell.
I hear Grandma Shirley call out,
"Nobody lives at the top of the Eiffel Tower,
but they used to!"
   "Thanks!" I call back as I run up another flight.
   I knock on Great-Grandma Lee's door.

"Got a question?" asks Great-Grandma Lee.
"Can art be invisible?" I ask.
"Is anything brighter than yellow?
Are those macaroons?"

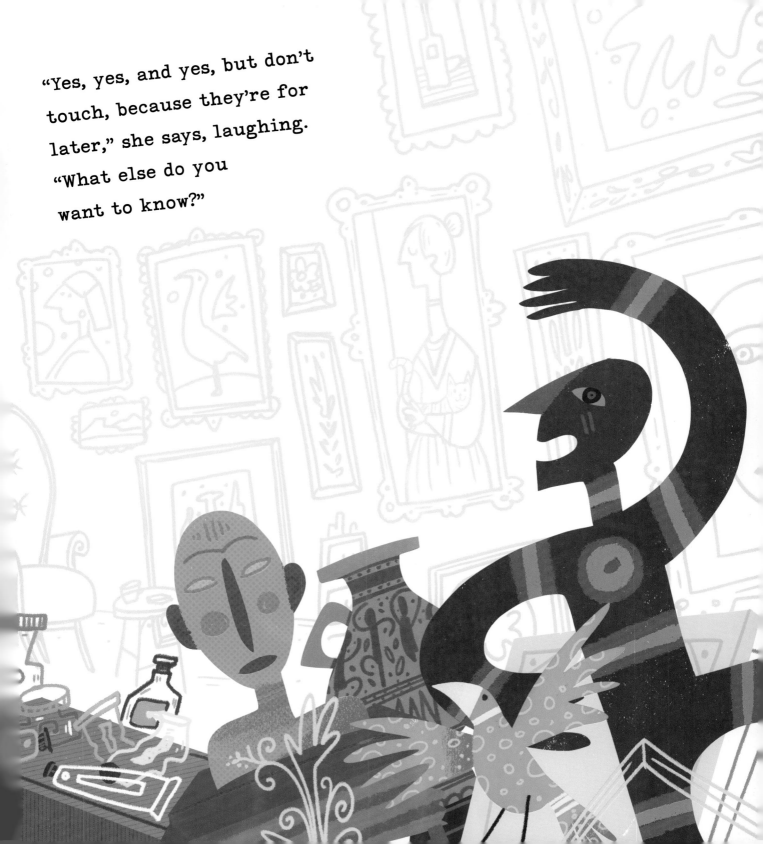

"Yes, yes, and yes, but don't touch, because they're for later," she says, laughing. "What else do you want to know?"

"Why do you cut off both ends of a roast?" I ask.

Great-Grandma Lee smiles.

"Why do you think?"

"Because they look all wobbly?" I say.

"No," says Great-Grandma Lee. "Here's a clue: they *had* to be cut off."

"Because they were naughty?" I ask.

"Nope," says Great-Grandma Lee.
"Here's another clue: They were
too big for their own good."

## "Because they would've exploded?"

I ask.

"Probably not," says Great-Grandma Lee. "Here's your last clue: They needed their own space."

I think that over. *The ends had to be cut off. They were too big. And they needed their own space...*

*I've got it!*

Great-Grandma Lee grins.

"Because if I didn't cut off the ends,
the roast wouldn't fit in my pan!"

**"Ah-HA!"** I say.

"I'm glad you asked," says Great-Grandma Lee. "You know what happens to people who don't ask questions?"

"They get boring?" I ask.

"Yes! They get stuck on one answer. When I'm painting, I ask questions all the time. Like, how can I make this bolder? Or brighter? Or better?"

I know why Grandma Shirley and Mom didn't ask about the roast . . . They forgot that even old recipes can have new questions.

"I'll never stop asking questions!"

At our seder, I ask the four questions, which come down to one big one: "Why is this night different from all other nights?"

מַה נִּשְׁתַּנָּה...

# I think I've got the answer!

"Is it because on Passover we cook together, we set the table, and we ask questions together? It's like we're all connected."

"Those aren't the *official* reasons," says Great-Grandma Lee, "but they're great reasons. Got another question?"
*Definitely!*

"What makes sidewalks crack?

"hy do elevators count oors and not ceilings?

Is the country of Greece really greasy?"

# What do you want to know *right now?*

"Next year, can I eat the
ends of the roast?"

"Yes!"

everyone answers.